Reycraft Books
145 Huguenot Street
New Rochelle, NY 10801

Reycraftbooks.com

Reycraft Books is a trade imprint and trademark of Newmark Learning, LLC.

This edition is published by arrangement with Native Realities Publishing.
© Native Realities Publishing

Native Realities, LLC
Publisher/CEO - Lee Francis IV CCO - Aaron Cuffee
Program Director - Jasmine Cuffee
INC Comics
Artistic Director - Arigon Starr

All rights reserved. No portion of this book may be reproduced, stored in a retrieval system, or transmitted in any form or by any means, electronic, mechanical, photocopying, recording, or otherwise, without written permission from the publisher. For information regarding permission, please contact info@reycraftbooks.com.

Educators and Librarians: Our books may be purchased in bulk for promotional, educational, or business use. Please contact sales@reycraftbooks.com.

This is a work of fiction. Names, characters, places, dialogue, and incidents described either are the product of the author's imagination or are used fictitiously. Any resemblance to actual persons, living or dead, is entirely coincidental.

Sale of this book without a front cover or jacket may be unauthorized. If this book is coverless, it may have been reported to the publisher as "unsold or destroyed" and may have deprived the author and publisher of payment.

Library of Congress Cataloging-in-Publication Data is available.

ISBN: 978-1-4788-6808-8

Printed in Dongguan, China. 8557/0224/20987

10 9 8 7 6 5 4

First Edition Paperback published by Reycraft Books 2019

Reycraft Books and Newmark Learning, LLC. support diversity and the First Amendment, and celebrate the right to read.

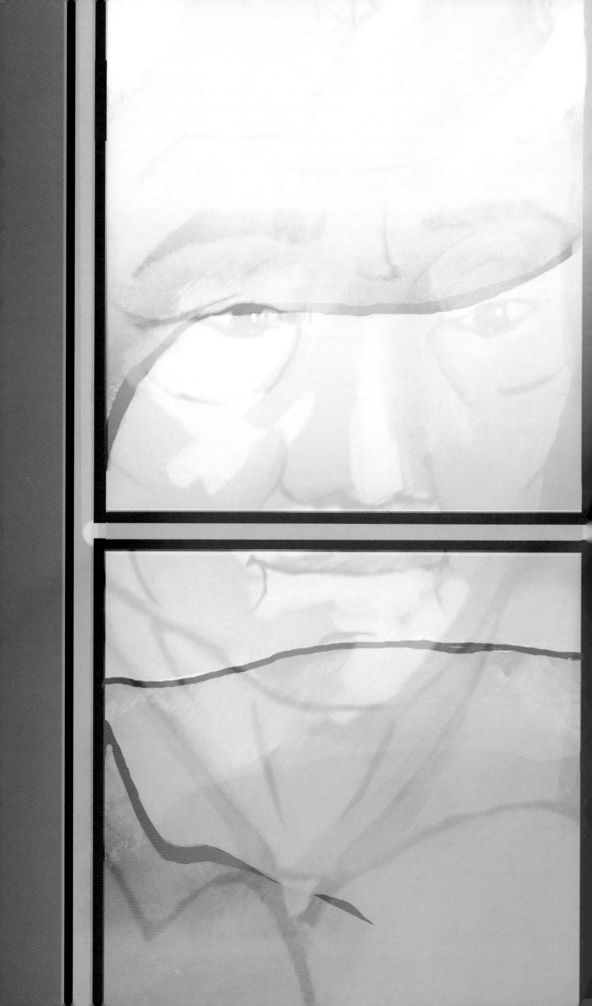

TALES OF THE
MIGHTY
CODE TALKERS

To those fathers, brothers, sisters,
moms, aunties, uncles and cousins who
have served and continue to serve.

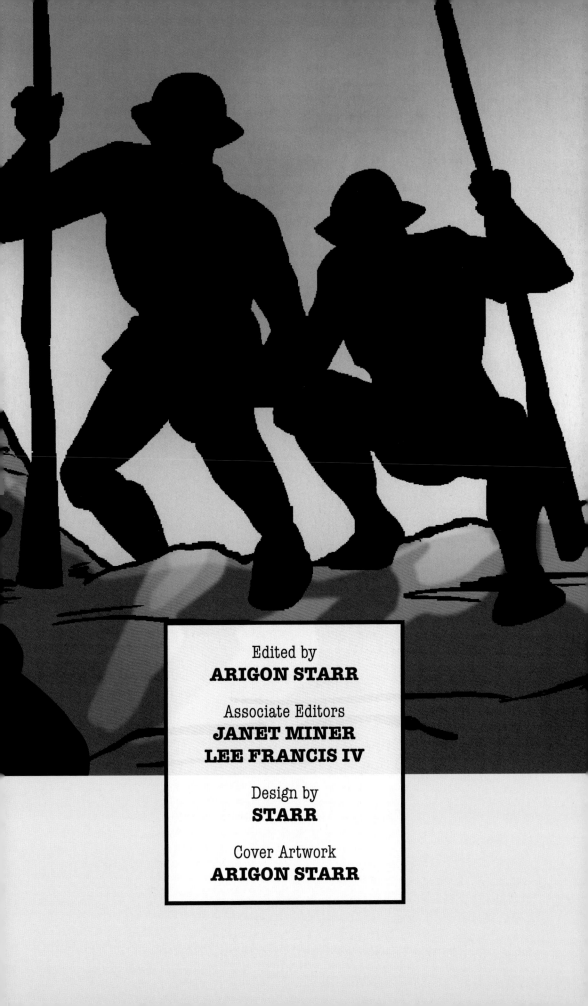

Edited by
ARIGON STARR

Associate Editors
JANET MINER
LEE FRANCIS IV

Design by
STARR

Cover Artwork
ARIGON STARR

TABLE OF CONTENTS

Prologue 3

We Speak in Secret 7

Annumpa Luma: Code Talker 21

PFC Joe 35

Epilogue 49

The History of Code Talkers 54

Biographies 56

PROLOGUE: HOMEPLACE

WORDS
LEE FRANCIS III

ART
ARIGON STARR

WHERE THE MORNING SUN FIRST TOUCHES THE LAND OF THE PEOPLE

I START ON A JOURNEY TO THE PLACE OF BEGINNING

RETURN TO THE HOMEPLACE
ON GRANDMOTHER SPIDER'S WEB.

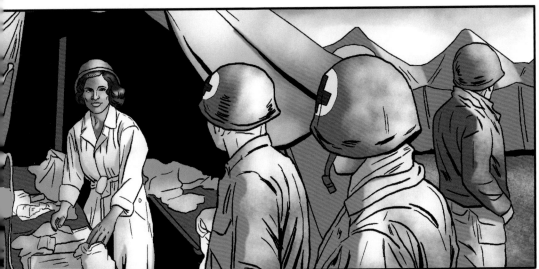

RETURN TO THE HOMEPLACE
TO THE PEOPLE OF THE
WHITE LAKE

RETURN TO THE HOMEPLACE
WITH GIFTS AND STORIES

RETURN TO THE HOMEPLACE

"WE SPEAK IN SECRET"

Story, Art, Colors, Letters
by
Roy Boney, Jr.

"BEING SURROUNDED BY DEATH AND DESTRUCTION IS SOMETHING NO ONE EVER GETS USED TO."

I STILL DON'T GET HOW THEY MANAGE TO KEEP SHELLING US SO ACCURATELY, MOUSE!

BACK HOME, DAD ALWAYS SAID, "WHEN YOU TALK TOO MUCH, EVEN THE MOUNTAINS WILL KNOW YOUR BUSINESS..."

"EVERY EXPLOSION WAS LIKE A DEATH RATTLE UNDER OUR FEET."

...SO IT SEEMS TO ME, RUNNY, THAT SOMEONE HERE HAS BEEN TALKING.

SURELY YOU DON'T THINK WE HAVE SP---

"ON THAT PARTICULAR DAY I THOUGHT IT WAS MY TIME TO WALK ON."

"A BIG BERTHA AIMED SQUARELY AT OUR BUNKER NEARLY DID US IN. IT RAINED SHELLS THAT WEIGHED OVER ONE THOUSAND KILOS ON US."

K-ZZZZZK...WHAT... KZZZZK...GOING ON... KZZK...DO YOU COPY??

"AT FIRST I COULDN'T HEAR. IT TOOK A BIT TO GET REORIENTED."

TOP SECRET

"ANNUMPA LUMA: CODE TALKER"

Story, Art, Colors, Letters
by
Arigon Starr

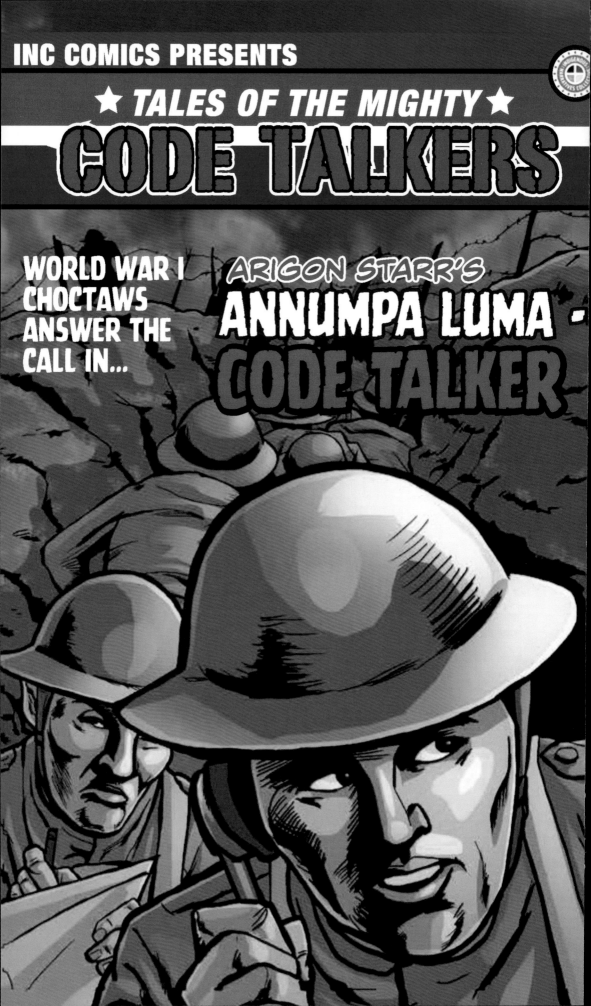

TIME PASSED QUICKER WHEN WE CHOCTAWS COULD SPEND TIME TOGETHER, TALKING IN OUR *FORBIDDEN* LANGUAGE.

I LIKE SOLOMON'S IDEA.

THE BRASS MIGHT NOT. I SURE GOT A LICKIN' FOR SPEAKIN' CHOCTAW AT SCHOOL.

WHILE ME, MITCHELL, OTIS AND ALBERT TALKED ABOUT OUR DARING PLAN, WE DIDN'T NOTICE CAPTAIN LAWRENCE LISTENING IN.

THOSE MEN --

WHAT *LANGUAGE* IS *THAT?*

SIR . . .

ENTER THE CHOCTAW WHO KILLED SEVENTY-NINE GERMANS AND CAPTURED ONE HUNDRED AND SEVENTY-ONE OF THEM ALMOST BY *HIMSELF.* . .

JOSEPH OKLAHOMBI.

CAPTAIN LAWRENCE WOULD HAVE PUT ANYONE ELSE IN JAIL FOR JUST *TOUCHIN'* HIM!

CAPTAIN, THE MEN WERE TALKING ABOUT A PLAN TO *WIN THE WAR.*

WE'D BEEN TRYIN' TO CAPTURE A BIG RAIL LINK IN THE GERMAN SUPPLY LINES FOR WEEKS. THEY'D BEEN SHOOTIN' OUR MESSENGERS, TAPPIN' OUR LINES AND BREAKIN' OUR CODES.

OUT OF IDEAS, THE BRASS WERE *FINALLY* WILLING TO HEAR OURS.

WHEN I HEARD THESE MEN SPEAK IN THEIR NATIVE TONGUE, IT GAVE ME AN IDEA. . .

THEIR LANGUAGE ISN'T WRITTEN DOWN.

IT'S NOT LATIN-BASED.

IT'S CHOCTAW.

IT HAS TWENTY-SIX DIALECTS.

THE GERMANS WILL *NEVER* CRACK IT.

IMPRESSIVE, CAPTAIN.

CORPORAL, TELL ME *YOUR* PLAN.

YOU GIVE US THE MESSAGES, WE SEND 'EM IN CHOCTAW.

HMPH! EXACTLY HOW MANY CHOCTAWS ARE IN MY BATTALION? ARE THERE ANY AT HEADQUARTERS?

SIR, THERE ARE EIGHT SPEAKERS HERE AND TWO AT HQ - CARTERBY AND MAYTUBBY.

CORPORAL LOUIS, GET THOSE MEN ON THE PHONE. LET'S SEE WHAT YOU CHOCTAW BOYS CAN DO.

THE CAPTAIN WAS AS NERVOUS AS I WAS. WE *BOTH* WANTED THIS TO WORK.

PRIVATE BOBB, TELL THEM WE NEED MORE... COFFEE.

⟨HEY, BUDDY! WE NEED MORE COFFEE!⟩

CAPTAIN. . . HEADQUARTERS CONFIRMS AND DENIES OUR REQUEST FOR MORE COFFEE.

LET'S GO GET THOSE HUNS!

THE HAPPINESS WE INDIANS FELT AT BEING HEARD GAVE WAY TO A NEW FRUSTRATION.

NO CHOCTAW WORD FOR ARTILLERY? BATTALION? MACHINE GUN?

ARROWS... SCALPS.. HMM...

EVEN IF THERE WERE, SIR, THE GERMANS MIGHT STILL FIGURE IT OUT.

GRAINS OF CORN... HUHH..MMM...

OTIS AND ALBERT WERE ONTO SOMETHING. A BATTALION COULD BE A SINGLE GRAIN OF CORN.

A GRENADE COULD BE... A STONE.

A GROUP OF MANY SCOUTS... A PATROL.

WITH A CODE THAT WORKED IN OUR LANGUAGE, I WAS SENT TO HEADQUARTERS TO BE THE LEAD PERSON IN A BRAND NEW WAY TO BEAT BACK THE HUNS!

ON THE LAND OR SEA, AMERICAN INDIANS OUT VOLUNTEERED EVERY OTHER GROUP TO JOIN THE WAR.

WE WEREN'T EVEN *OFFICIAL U.S. CITIZENS.*

THAT WOULDN'T COME TIL' LATER.

WE HAD MADE GREAT STRIDES. OUR CODE GAVE US THE ELEMENT OF SURPRISE. OUR BOYS HAD THE HUNS ON THE RUN.

⟨THE THIRD BATTALION IS SENDING MORE ARTILLERY AND AMMUNITION. HANG ON, JOHNSON!⟩

⟨CAN'T COME SOON ENOUGH, SOLOMON!⟩

ZIIIING

KABLAM

NOEL JOHNSON, ONE OF OUR OWN, WAS KILLED IN ACTION.

HIS WORDS AND BRAVERY SAVED MANY LIVES.

NOVEMBER 11, 1918.

TWO WEEKS AFTER WE STARTED USING OUR LANGUAGE -- OUR CODE...

THE GERMANS *SURRENDERED.*

AS THE FELLAS CELEBRATED, I THOUGHT ABOUT MY FALLEN COMRADES....MY HOME.

I THOUGHT ABOUT THE TEACHERS AT INDIAN BOARDING SCHOOL WHO PUNISHED ME FOR SPEAKING CHOCTAW.

HERE'S TO MISBEHAVIN'!

THE ARMY BRASS ACKNOWLEDGED OUR EFFORTS AND TOLD US TO EXPECT WIDE RECOGNITION AND MEDALS.

AFTER A FEW MONTHS, THEY TOLD US TO KEEP WHAT WE DID...*SECRET.*

OUR "THANKS"...

...A TINY PARADE THROUGH TOWN.

WHEN THE ARMY ASKED ME FOR MY NEXT OF KIN, I SAID IT WAS HER.

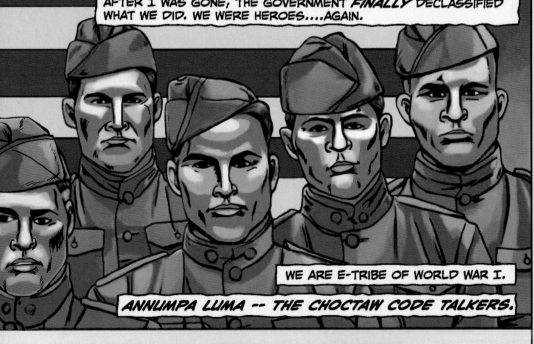

AFTER I WAS GONE, THE GOVERNMENT *FINALLY* DECLASSIFIED WHAT WE DID. WE WERE HEROES....AGAIN.

WE ARE E-TRIBE OF WORLD WAR I.

ANNUMPA LUMA -- THE CHOCTAW CODE TALKERS.

"PFC JOE"

Words, Art, Colors
by
Jonathan Nelson

Additional Colors, Letters
by
Arigon Starr

PFC JOE

MILITARY MEANING	NAVAJO PRONUNCIATION	NAVAJO MEANING
Battalion	Tacheene	Red Soil
Company		Mexican
Pl...		

	Teldi-noy-ye-mk		
Submarine	9eer-lo		Iron Fish

JONATHAN NELSON

FIDENTIAL

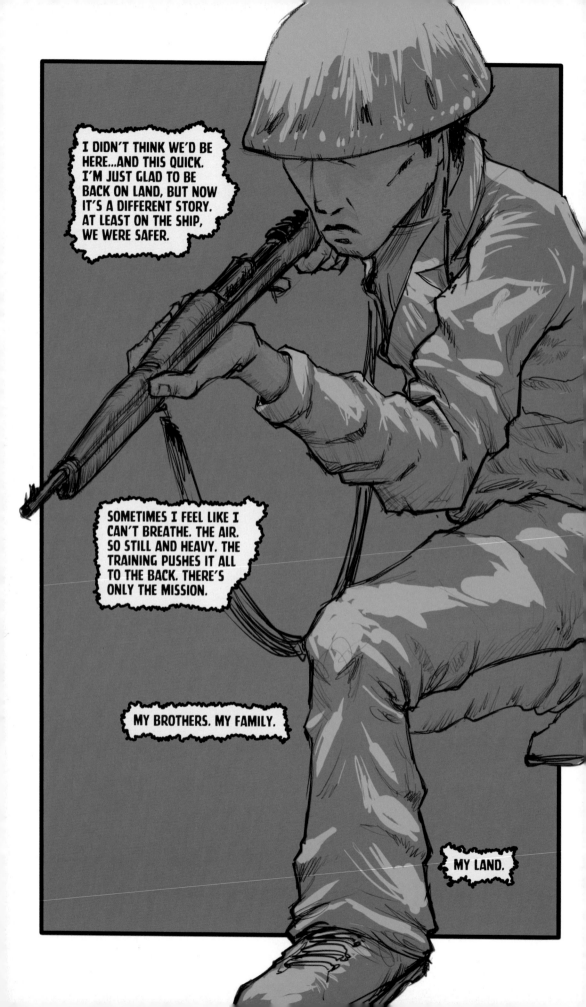

LESSONS BEGIN AT BIRTH AND WE NEVER STOP LEARNING.
AS KIDS, WE LEARN FROM FAMILY. FROM WATCHING. AND EVEN PLAYING.
WE EVEN LEARN FROM JOHN WAYNE.

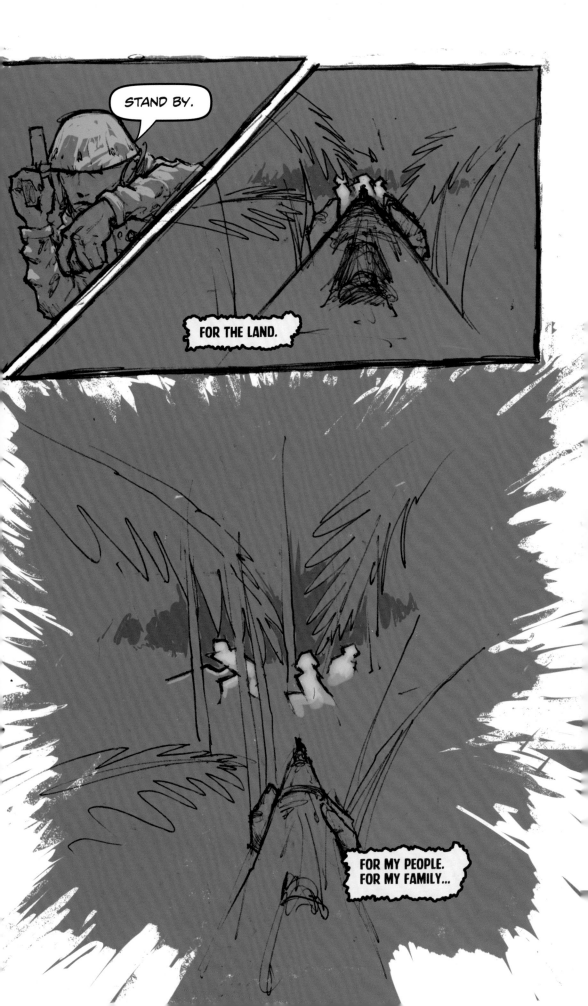

EPILOGUE:
LEGACY

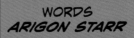

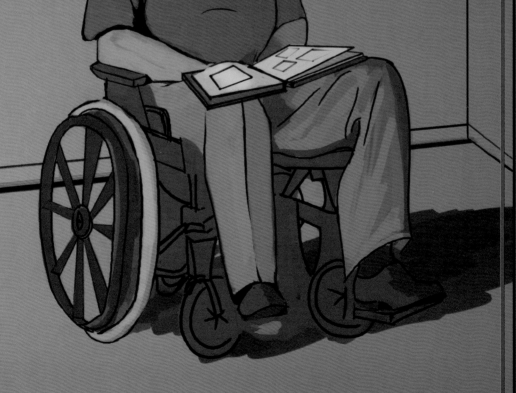

I REMEMBER.

WHEN I WAS A BOY, I DIDN'T KNOW A WORD OF ENGLISH. WANTED TO LEARN. KNEW IT MEANT A GOOD JOB, A GOOD LIVING FOR MY FAMILY.

AT BOOT CAMP, CULTURES COLLIDED.

IT WASN'T EASY, BUT I MET THOSE CHALLENGES.

OUR CULTURE AND LANGUAGE DEFEATED THE ENEMY.

THE HISTORY OF THE CODE TALKERS
By Lee Francis IV

Native American nations have always fought to defend themselves. Anyone who threatened their families, cultures, and lands was their enemy, including the United States. As a result of wars with the United States, many tribes were forced off their lands, relocated, or confined to reservations where they endured poverty, racism, and attempts to erase their traditional cultures. Languages were particularly targeted in the government's efforts to change Native American ways of life.

Beginning in the late 1800s, Indian children were forbidden to speak their own languages and were punished in government and church supported boarding schools if they did. Most Native Americans were not legally considered citizens of the United States until 1924. Even then, some states refused to let American Indians vote until the 1950s.

Despite this, many Native American men and women have served, and continue to serve, in all branches of the military. In every conflict and war Native Americans have honorably defended their homelands and the United States.

During World War I and World War II, hundreds of Native Americans joined the United States armed forces and used words from their traditional tribal languages as weapons.

The United States military asked them to develop secret battle communications based on their languages. "Code Talkers," as they came to be known after World War II, are warriors and heroes who were instrumental in the victories of the United States and its allies.

Code Talking was pioneered in World War I by the Cherokee and Choctaw tribal members who transmitted battle messages in their tribal languages by telephone. Although not used extensively, the World War I telephone squads played a key role in helping the United States Army win several battles in France that brought about the end of the war.

Beginning in 1940, the Army recruited Comanches, Choctaws, Hopis, Cherokees, and others to transmit messages. The Army had special American Indian recruiters working to find Comanches in Oklahoma who would enlist.

The Marine Corps recruited Navajo Code Talkers in 1941 and 1942. Philip Johnston was a World War I veteran who had heard about the successes of the Choctaw telephone squad. Johnston, although not Native, had grown up on the Navajo reservation. In 1942, he suggested to the Marine Corps that Navajos and other tribes could be very helpful in maintaining communications secrecy. After viewing a demonstration of messages sent in the Navajo language, the Marine Corps was so impressed that they recruited 30 Navajos in two weeks to develop a code within their language.

After the Navajo code was developed, the Marine Corps established a Code Talking school. As the war progressed, more than 400 Navajos were eventually recruited as Code Talkers. The training was intense. Following their basic training, the Code Talkers completed extensive training in communications and memorizing the code.

Some Code Talkers enlisted, others were drafted. Many of the Code Talkers who served were under age and had to lie about their age to join. Some were just 15 years old. Through the course of World War II and the Korean and Vietnam Wars, America's enemies never deciphered any of these coded messages. Ultimately, there were Code Talkers from at least 16 tribes who served in the Army, the Marines, and the Navy including Assiniboine, Cherokee, Choctaw, Comanche, Meskwaki, Navajo, Lakota, and Seminole.

Without the contribution of these brave Americans, history may have taken a very different course. Despite the tragic history of colonization, conquest, genocide, forced relocation, reservations and assimilation, Native Americans have chosen to serve the United States in every time of conflict.

Which begs the question ... "Why?" Why fight to defend a country that has failed for so long to respect and protect the lives and rights of Indigenous people?

Perhaps it is best stated by the soldier who was the last surviving original member of the Navajo Code Talkers and who lived to be a recipient of the Congressional Gold Medal:

"People ask me, 'Why did you go? Look at all the mistreatment that has been done to your people.' Somebody's got to go, somebody's got to defend this country. Somebody's got to defend the freedom. This is the reason why I went. My wartime experiences developing a code that utilized the Navajo language taught how important our Navajo culture is to our country. For me that is the central lesson: that diverse cultures can make a country richer and stronger."
Corporal Chester Nez, USMC, Retired

BIOGRAPHIES

ARIGON STARR

is an enrolled member of the Kickapoo Tribe of Oklahoma, and a multi-talented and award-winning musician, actor, playwright and artist. Her comic Super Indian was originally produced as a nationally broadcast radio comedy series in 2007 and became a webcomic that debuted in 2011. In 2012, she published Super Indian Volume One, followed by Volume Two in 2015. The Healthy Aboriginal Network tapped her to create key illustrations for the United Nations Rights of the Child poster set targeted to an indigenous audience. She is a contributor to the award winning comic anthology MOONSHOT: The Indigenous Comic Collection and is a founder of the Indigenous Narratives Collective (INC), a group of Native American comic book writers and artists. Arigon's comic work has also been featured in several pop culture art museum exhibits, including the Heard Museum in Phoenix, Arizona, Museum of Indian Arts and Culture in Santa Fe, New Mexico, and the Department of the Interior in Washington, DC. Starr is based in Los Angeles and continues her work on Super Indian. Visit Arigon on line at arigonstarr.com or Super Indian at superindiancomics.com.

LEE FRANCIS IV

is the Founder of Native Realities and the current director of Wordcraft Circle of Native Writers and Storytellers. He is the writer for Sixkiller (December 2016) and Pueblo Jones (Summer 2017). His previous work has appeared in numerous journals, anthologies, and books and he has received several awards for his scholarship around Indigenous education. Dr. Francis is an award-winning slam poet (UNM, 2008) and has toured the US extensively as a performer. He lives in the Southwest with his fantastic family where they spend time playing games and catching up on comic books!

WESHOYOT ALVITRE

is a Tongva/Scots-Gaelic illustrator, comic artist, and illustrator. She has a BA in Fine Art and Illustration and has been creating comics for the last decade. Weshoyot's work appears in the Eisner Award winning books Umbrella Academy #6 (Dark Horse), Little Nemo: Dream Another Dream (Locust Moon) and the upcoming Moonshot Volume 2 (AH). Her art can be seen online at www.facebook.com/weshoyot and #weshoyot on Instagram and Twitter. She resides in California with her husband, dual kids, and two cats.

ROY BONEY, JR.

ᎠᎣᏍ ᎠᏫᏆ (Roy Boney, Jr.) is a full blood citizen of the ᏣᏪᎩ ᎅᏃᏨ Cherokee Nation. He lives in Tahlequah, Oklahoma. He is an award-winning artist and writer. He has a BFA in Graphic Design from Oklahoma State University and a MA in Studio Art from the University of Arkansas Little Rock. He is co-creator and illustrator on the comic book series Dead Eyes Open for Slave Labor Graphics. Other projects include contributing stories to Native Graphic Classics and the Eisner Award nominated anthology Trickster: Native American Tales. He also has contributed art & articles about Cherokee art, language, and culture to First American Art Magazine, Native Peoples, Oklahoma Today, and Indian Country Today. He currently works in the Cherokee Language Program at Cherokee Nation in Tahlequah, Oklahoma.

RENEE NEJO

is a freelance artist, illustrator, writer, and independent game designer who has worked on games like Ever Jane, Gravity Ghost, and most recently her own project Blood Quantum. Based out of Colorado, Renee is a tribal member of the Mesa Grande Band of Mission Indians and an unapologetic advocate for education and the self determination of the Native American people. She is also currently a volunteer mentor for at-risk youth at Thomas Jefferson High School in Denver.

JONATHAN NELSON

is Dine (Navajo) and was born and raised in the Four Corners area of New Mexico. Jonathan, or Johnny, as he prefers, began his art experience as a child with coloring books. His drawing has evolved into a career as a creative professional. When he's not painting or drawing, he is designing print material and websites as a graphic artist. In his youth, he collected comic books and started tracing famous comic book characters like Spiderman and The X-Men. Elementary tracing evolved into freehand drawings with No. 2 school pencils. Nowadays, he works in ballpoint pen. Enter the world of Jonesy the sheep. His work is inspired from identity and life on the Navajo reservation. The Wool of Jonesy begins when he wakes one warm spring morning to shave himself and tries to sell his brown wool at a local trading post. The humorous narrative brings to light the sustaining life of indigenous culture and its ongoing struggle in a Eurocentric society.

"Who would think that a bunch of sheep herders would create a code that no one in the world could break?"

Dr. Sam Billison, Navajo Code Talker

"I always wonder why it took so long to recognize us for what we did ... They [his deceased comrades] are not here to enjoy what I'm getting after all these years. Yes, it's been a long, long time."

Charles Chibitty, Comanche Code Talker

"The two [Choctaw] soldiers who were overheard by the officer probably thought they were in trouble rather than about to provide the answer to the army's communication problems."

Judy Allen, Choctaw Nation of Oklahoma

"The language which they forbade me to speak is the language that saved this country."

Gilbert Horn, Sr., Assiniboine Code Talker